P9-CFC-004

Apprentices,

By the time you find this letter, I will be gone. An important quest has called me away, and I'm afraid I do not know when I may return. But do not imagine that my sudden departure means your apprenticeships have come to an end. Quite the contrary, my friends. Had I not left, our final course would have begun—a session on the monsters who inhabit our world. Any wizard worth a spell pouch knows the habits and habitats of these beasts backward and forward, and I expect no less of you.

And so I leave you with this volume. The monsters described in this book aren't the kind that you once feared hid under your bed. No, my friends, these monsters are quite real. They walk our city's streets in the dead of night. They wait alongside well-traveled paths. Some of them, I dare say, live among us in disguise. Not all monsters need be feared, however. There are many who live among us in peace, and some still who enjoy helping our kind.

This volume will have to substitute for the fascinating lectures you've come to anticipate from me. I expect you to read it and learn well. Only then will you be prepared to take on the robes of a true wizard and to defend yourself on a quest of your own.

Farewell,

Zendric

# A Practical Guide to MONSTERS

Inscribed by

*Zendric*

High Wizard and Master of Magic

MIRRORSTONE

# MONSTER PROTECTION

B efore beginning any quest in which you might encounter monsters, you must gather the proper equipment. Some of the basics include:

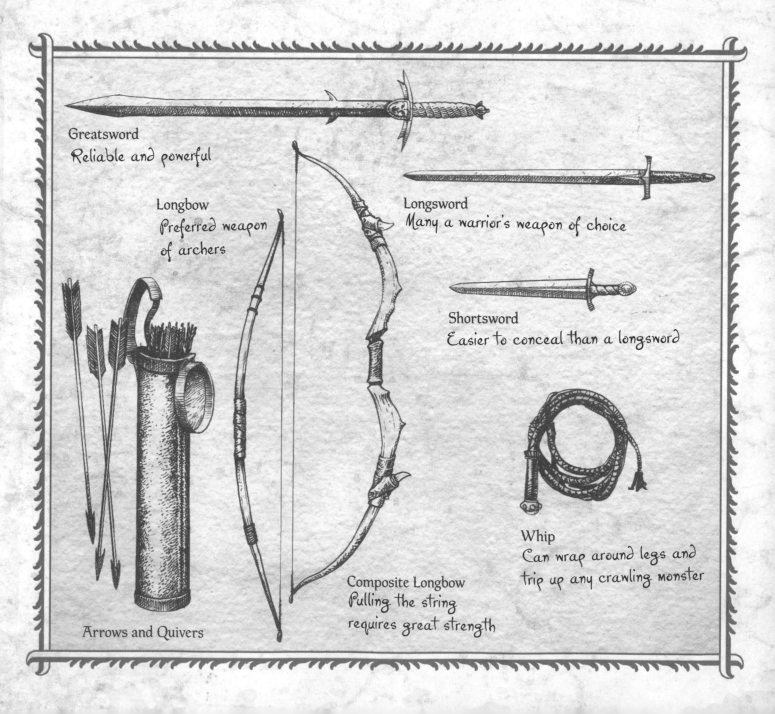

**Greatsword**
Reliable and powerful

**Longbow**
Preferred weapon of archers

**Longsword**
Many a warrior's weapon of choice

**Shortsword**
Easier to conceal than a longsword

**Whip**
Can wrap around legs and trip up any crawling monster

**Composite Longbow**
Pulling the string requires great strength

Arrows and Quivers

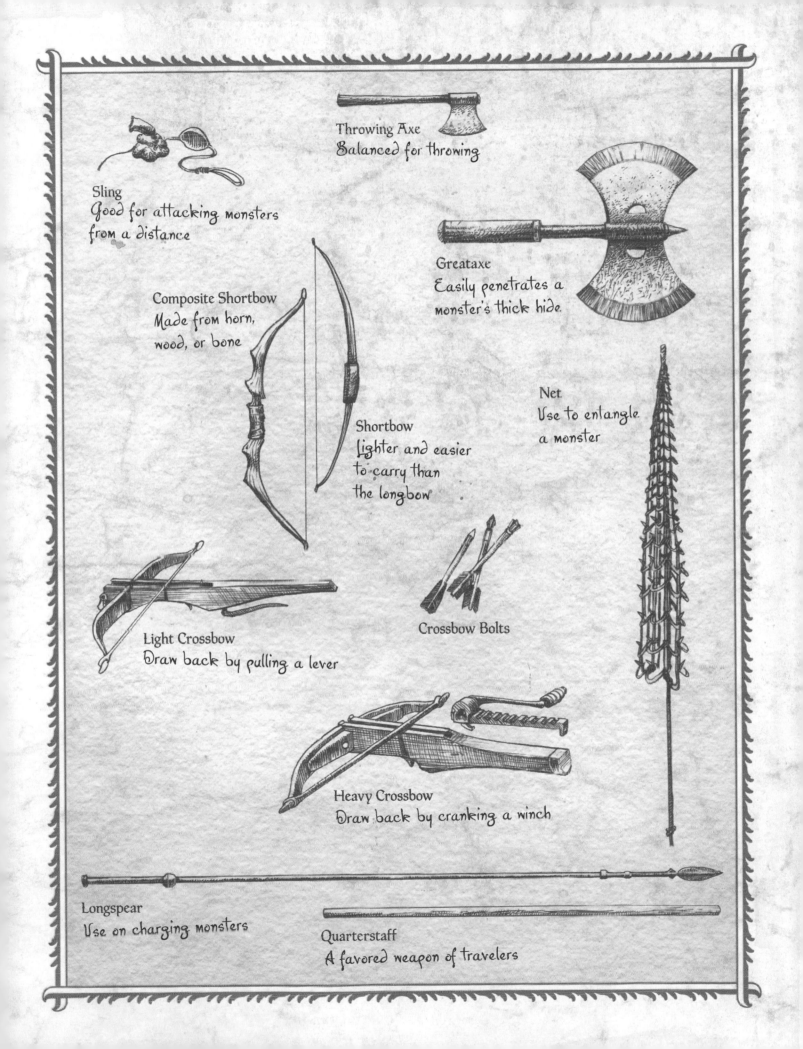

Throwing Axe
Balanced for throwing

Sling
Good for attacking monsters
from a distance

Greataxe
Easily penetrates a
monster's thick hide.

Composite Shortbow
Made from horn,
wood, or bone

Net
Use to entangle
a monster

Shortbow
Lighter and easier
to carry than
the longbow

Light Crossbow
Draw back by pulling a lever

Crossbow Bolts

Heavy Crossbow
Draw back by cranking a winch

Longspear
Use on charging monsters

Quarterstaff
A favored weapon of travelers

Bony protrusions

Faceted eyes

Wide mouth with jagged teeth

Soft underbelly

When attacking, the beast beats its wings, rears back, then snaps forward and strikes.

# Creepy Crawlers

All vicious hunters, these creepy, crawling beasts scuttle under and over the ground, searching for prey.

## Remorhaz

Next time you cross a frozen field, beware! There could be a monster lurking beneath your feet.

Remorhazes spend most of their lives burrowing tunnels beneath glacial ice. When they hear prey approaching, they burst onto the surface in a shower of ice and snow.

*A remorhaz's intestines hold a liquid called thrym. Thrym is so hot, it makes the creature's back glow red. Any weapon will be melted instantly by the heat.*

*But it will eat humans and frost giants*

### Remorhaz Facts

| | |
|---|---|
| Maximum Height | 20 feet |
| Maximum Weight | 10,000 pounds |
| Habitat | Snowy plains |
| Society | Tends to live alone |
| Diet | Mostly deer, elk, and polar bears |
| Language | Roaring, bellowing, howling |
| Attack methods | Swallow whole |
| Best defense | Weapons may be destroyed when they hit it—so use archery, spells, and acid flasks |

*Insectoid legs*

Flat, arctic wasteland

Entry

Entry

Entry

Entry

Smoothly
rounded
tunnel

Contains icy
stalactites

Central Chamber
About only twice the size of
the remorhaz

# TYPICAL REMORHAZ LAIR
Size of lair varies with size of creature

The remorhaz tends to live alone in tunnels carved out of rock and ice. The slippery tunnels can be lethal—made so slick because the heat of the beast's back causes the walls to melt. Then they freeze again, dangerously slicker than ever.

Once every year, in late summer, a remorhaz will find a mate. The pair lives together for about two months, until their babies hatch.

The female remorhaz lays only one or two eggs each year. She must coil around them and keep them warm at all times. If the eggs are left out in the cold for even one moment, they will not hatch.

Once hatched, a young remorhaz grows quickly. It will be ready to leave the nest after only four months.

# Thri-kreen

Thri-kreen are giant, intelligent insects that hunt in packs. Taller than a human man, the thri-kreen stands upright on two segmented legs. Its other four limbs end in four-fingered hands.

These giant insects might wear clothing or harnesses to carry gear, but they never wear armor. Their hard, sandy-yellow shells provide plenty of protection.

The thri-kreen's favorite weapon is called a gythka: a pole with a double blade at each end. If it can get close enough, it will bite its attackers, delivering a toxic venom that leaves the victim unable to move.

## THRI-KREEN FACTS

| | |
|---|---|
| Maximum Height | 7 feet |
| Maximum Weight | 200 pounds |
| Habitat | Deserts and savannahs |
| Society | Lives alone but hunts in packs |
| Diet | Animals and elves |
| Language | Thri-kreen language, some Common |
| Attack methods | Paralyzing venom, Gythka weapon |
| Best defense | Attack from a distance with a bow or a whip |

## ANKHEG FACTS

| | |
|---|---|
| Maximum Height | 10 feet |
| Maximum Weight | 800 pounds |
| Habitat | Tropical plains and forests |
| Society | Cluster |
| Diet | Can eat decayed organic matter but prefers fresh meat |
| Language | None |
| Attack methods | Squirt acid |
| Best defense | Stick it in place with a tanglefoot bag! |

To ward off predators, the ankheg secretes a stinky scent that has the odor of rotten fruit.

# Ankheg

The ankheg looks like a worm with many legs. It has sharp hooks on the end of each leg for burrowing, and its giant mandibles could chop down a small tree with one bite.

When prowling for food, the ankheg burrows into the ground, lying five or ten feet below the surface. When its sensitive antennae detects something approaching, it bursts out of the ground. After grabbing the unlucky creature in its mandibles, the ankheg squirts acid on its prey until the victim dissolves.

Like an insect, the ankheg can only grow bigger by shedding its exoskeleton. The process begins when it is two years old. For two long days, the ankheg struggles to escape from its hard shell. When it emerges at last, it is weak and easily defeated. While it waits for its new shell to grow, the beast hides in a deep tunnel.

# Phase Spider

Phase spiders are giant, magical eight-legged creatures with silver-white eyes. A dangerous hunter, this creature uses teleportation to surprise its victims.

A phase spider bides its time in warm, hilly areas and forbidden ruins, awaiting passing adventurers. When it senses prey approaching, it can use its magical abilities to hop into another plane, thereby becoming invisible. When the victim least expects it, the spider returns to our world and delivers its poisonous bite.

## PHASE SPIDER FACTS

| | |
|---|---|
| Maximum Height | 8 feet |
| Maximum Weight | 700 pounds |
| Habitat | Warm hills |
| Society | Lives alone or in clusters of two to five |
| Diet | Meat-eater |
| Language | None |
| Attack methods | Poisonous bite |
| Best defense | Use a ghost touch weapon |

## Bulette

*It will even eat treasure chests and sacks of gold.*

The bulette lives to eat. Like many other crawling beasts, it burrows underground to catch its prey by surprise. When it senses vibrations, it erupts through the surface and consumes its victim whole.

The bulette is a wanderer, with no lair and no particular habitat to call its own. When it enters an area, nothing is safe from its monstrous appetite. Even larger beasts such as ogres, trolls, and giants flee from its path.

### BULETTE FACTS

| | |
|---|---|
| Maximum Height | 15 feet |
| Maximum Weight | 16 tons |
| Habitat | Almost anywhere |
| Society | Normally lives alone but occasionally lives with a mate |
| Diet | Anything edible, with two exceptions: elves and dwarves |
| Language | None |
| Attack methods | Pounces on victims from underground |
| Best defense | Climb a tree and fire down from above! |

Griffons attack with foreclaws and beak.
They are especially accurate with their beak
attack, but if they hit you with both foreclaws,
they can rake you with their back claws.

Light golden feathers from its wing
tips to its razor sharp beak

Wingspan can exceed 25 feet

Tawny fur coats the griffon's back

Head of an eagle

Body of a lion

Powerful, muscular rear legs

A mere brush of these sharp
talons can slice through the
steel armor of a knight

Keen sense of smell. Sharp eyesight
can spot prey from up to two miles
away, even in total darkness.

# FLYING FIENDS

**B**eware, my friends, the beasts that soar through the sky. They are majestic from a distance; once upon you, their evil knows no bounds.

## Griffon

There is no flying fiend more majestic than the griffon. Part lion, part eagle, it is a fierce hunter who will stop at nothing to secure its prey. Griffons prefer to dine on horses and other horselike beasts, but they have been known to attack riders and anything that stands between them and their future meals.

| GRIFFON FACTS | |
| --- | --- |
| Maximum Height | 5 feet at the shoulder |
| Maximum Weight | About 500 pounds |
| Habitat | Rocky caves near plains |
| Society | Prides |
| Diet | Horses and their kin-pegasi, unicorns, etc. |
| Language | Understands Common but cannot speak it |
| Attack methods | Prefer to pounce |
| Best defense | Lasso it or cast a net over it, so it has to come to ground and stay in one place |

Will screech like an eagle when excited (usually by a horse)

Like its cousin the lion, a griffon lives in a group called a pride. Each pride contains several mated pairs, some griffon fledglings, and a strong male leader. The pride inhabits shallow caves near each other on a rocky cliff.

Yes, the rumors are true: you can train a griffon as a mount. If properly trained, a griffon will fight to the death to protect its rider. Only griffons younger than three years old respond to human guidance; it is best to secure one before they've fled the nest. Obviously, this task must be undertaken with extreme caution. I have only known one hapless knight in my time who attempted to capture a griffon for training. He disappeared, never to be seen again.

Open plains

Cliff face

Shallow cave

Other griffons' lairs

Nest made of sticks and leaves

Nest located in shallow cave near other griffons' lairs

# TYPICAL GRIFFON LAIR
Size of lair varies with size of griffon

## Chimera Facts

| | |
|---|---|
| Maximum Height | 5 feet at the shoulder |
| Maximum Weight | 4,000 pounds |
| Habitat | Prefers warm hilly regions |
| Society | Some prefer solitude, others live in prides |
| Diet | Goat head browses on plants, while lion and dragon heads prefer flesh |
| Language | Draconic |
| Attack methods | Breath weapon depends on kind of dragon head |
| Best defense | Spread out! |

Black breathes a stream of acid, Blue shoots a bolt of lightning, Green spews a cloud of gas, Red spits flames, White expels blistering hail

Only attempt to fight this beast when in the company of other adventurers.

# Chimera

The chimera is a truly monstrous beast. Its hind end is like a goat's body, while its front paws are derived from a lion's. Its body bears wings like a large dragon. But most repellent of all, it has three heads: one like a goat's, the second like a lion's, and the third like a dragon's.

A chimera almost always launches a surprise attack from the sky, whipping up a whirlwind of teeth, horns, claws, and deadly breath weapons. If you are unlucky enough to encounter this beast with no friends to come to your aid, the best defense is to flee.

# Manticore

With the body of a lion, the wings of a dragon, and a vaguely human face, a manticore's appearance is enough to send shivers down the spines of the bravest adventurers. Its razor-sharp teeth and long claws are powerful, but they are not this creature's most fearsome weapon—that honor lies in the creature's tail. With a mere flick of its tail, the manticore can shoot a volley of deadly spikes.

Manticores mate for life and tend to have one or two cubs every few years. The cubs may seem harmless, but do not be fooled. Though they cannot fly or fling spikes like their parents, their bites are just as cruel.

## Manticore Facts

| | |
|---|---|
| Maximum Height | 10 feet |
| Maximum Weight | 1,000 pounds |
| Habitat | Typically lives in marshy areas, but can be found almost anywhere |
| Society | Lives alone, in pairs, or in prides |
| Diet | Any flesh, but their favorite food is humans |
| Language | Common |
| Attack methods | Tail spikes |
| Best defense | It can't change direction quickly; try to duck behind cover whenever it draws near, shooting at it from a distance |

# Yrthak

The yrthak is one of the strangest beasts I've encountered in my travels. It has no eyes, yet blindness does not stop this creature's relentless hunt. Instead it uses a special organ on its tongue to sense the movement and noises made by its prey.

As it flies through the sky, the yrthak's tongue dangles from its jaw until it comes across a worthy victim. Focusing energy to the horn atop its head, the yrthak unleashes a sound so loud it can knock a living being to the ground.

*Surprising considering their intelligence*

## YRTHAK FACTS

| | |
|---|---|
| Maximum Height | About 20 feet |
| Maximum Weight | 5,000 pounds |
| Habitat | Cool mountains |
| Society | Solitary or groups known as clutches |
| Diet | Anything but prefer fresh meat |
| Language | None |
| Attack methods | Sonic lance, explosion |
| Best defense | Avoid being snatched by its claws at all costs |

# Harpy

You'll smell this foul beast long before you see her, for a harpy never, ever bathes. With youthful—but hideous—features and a mouth full of rotten teeth, you'd never guess that a harpy's greatest weapon is her charming voice.

If you have the poor luck to encounter a harpy on your journeys, be certain to put wax in your ears before she begins to sing. If you don't, the harpy's song will so enthrall you that you will be unable to fight back as she drags you off.

A harpy can lay an egg every other year if she wishes, but harpies have no mothering instinct. Once hatched, the young must scavenge their own food—usually cave vermin and leftovers from the flight's last meal.

*I have never heard tell of a male harpy.*

## Harpy Facts

| | |
|---|---|
| Maximum Height | 6 feet |
| Maximum Weight | 150 pounds |
| Habitat | Caves along coastlines with shipping lanes; near well-traveled paths |
| Society | Flights of about six |
| Diet | All animals, but prefer humans or half-humans |
| Language | Native language made up of cackles and shrieks, can sing in Common |
| Attack methods | Song spell |
| Best defense | Bring a bard to counter the deadly song |

## Gargoyle Facts

| | |
|---|---|
| Maximum Height | 6 feet |
| Maximum Weight | 500 pounds |
| Habitat | Anywhere |
| Society | Solitary or groups called wings |
| Diet | None |
| Language | Common, Terran |
| Attack methods | Prefer to launch surprise attacks |
| Best defense | Use magic weapons |

Gargoyles first came to be as harmless spouts carved into the sides of buildings to funnel rain away from a structure's walls. Then a sorcerer concocted an enchantment that brought the sculptures to life.

## Gargoyle

Have you ever seen a stone statue perched on the side of a building? Are you absolutely sure it was a statue? It's very likely that stony beast was in fact one of the vilest flying fiends, known in wizarding circles as the gargoyle.

Gargoyles do not need to eat or drink, but do not assume these creatures pose no risk. In fact, gargoyles are all the more dangerous because their attacks are not limited by the size of their stomachs. Instead they attack simply to entertain themselves.

Gargoyles are well suited as guards in particular. They wait motionless above the threshold, assuming the face of a sculpture, until a visitor arrives at the door. Then, they swoop down to interrogate the guest. If you're unlucky enough to be deemed an unwanted visitor, be prepared to fight!

Medusas wear human clothing such as loose dresses or robes. They rarely wear armor and cannot wear helmets.

Hair a swarm of slithering snakes

Red-glowing eyes visible from a distance. When viewed from far away, they are often the only clue that you are dealing with a medusa.

Body and face appear human from a distance, but upon closer inspection the skin is scaly like a snake's.

Children of medusas grow at the same rate as humans.

Hatchlings are harmless until about two years old, when the serpentine hair comes to life. By the time the medusa reaches thirteen years of age, she will gain the power to petrify.

Carries a knife, dagger, or short bow

# Viperous Villains

These monsters slither and slide as they move in to attack, striking fear into the heart of even the greatest of warriors.

## Medusa

With one cruel glance, a medusa can best the sharpest sword, turning her enemy into stone. Averting your eyes is not enough to deter her attack. If you avoid looking at her, she will step forth and unleash her serpentine hair, capable of thousands of highly poisonous bites.

### Medusa Facts

| | |
|---|---|
| Maximum Height | 5 to 6 feet tall (snakes add another foot) |
| Maximum Weight | 150 pounds |
| Habitat | Can be found almost anywhere |
| Society | Solitary or covey of two to four |
| Diet | Large rodents and other small beasts |
| Language | Common |
| Attack methods | Petrifying gaze, poison |
| Best defense | Blind her! She can still turn people to stone, but it's hard to aim at what you can't see. |

Some dwell in cities and are involved in the criminal underground.

Where our ship
laid anchor ✗

Treasury

Shipwreck
Beach

Conservatory

Cave dwellings
where medusas live,
alone or in coveys,
dot the cliffs

Hall of Sculptures

Royal
Ovens

Palace

Serpent's Peak

Temple

# MEDUSA ISLAND

Medusas can be cruel creatures, but—like humans—they are not all the same. I learned this lesson as a young wizard, when I journeyed to Medusa Island. My fellows and I were foolish enough to believe we could enter the island undetected. I would have lost my life if not for the kindness of one medusa. I hope one day that I will have the chance to return the favor.

Day 24

Land ho! After many days at sea, my fellows and I have at last arrived at the legendary Medusa Island. Terina has devised an ingenious roping system that will allow us to climb the cliffs beneath the treasury without the guards spotting us. Come tomorrow, we will be back on the ship sailing for home, with more gold than we could have ever imagined.

Day 25

I write this from a dank cell in the bowels of the medusas' palace. Our confidence was, alas, the foolish tripe of youth. We were captured the moment our ship laid anchor beneath the cliffs. Strangely, once we were brought before the royal court, one of the royals—I believe her name is Ssarine—requested that I be named her personal slave. I do not hold much hope for my future. The medusas are known for their cruelty and do not have much use for humans, except on their dinner plates. My life may be spared for now, but I can only imagine what wicked tricks Ssarine has planned. I report to her quarters at daybreak.

Day 28

The most extraordinary thing has occurred of Ssarine, I find myself on a ship sailing moment I delivered her customary breakf

Here is a page torn out of my journal from that fateful trip

## ANTIDOTE FOR MEDUSA POISON

3 sprigs entwistle—ground into fine powder

2 ounces mother's root—grated

Echacia—add to boiling water, and simmer for ten to twenty minutes

Yam—boiled then strained

Two drops yew breath

3 black agate crystals

15 medusa tears

Combine all ingredients, properly prepared, in a flask. Place over an open flame for no more than thirty minutes. Intone the words

# Yuan-ti

Yuan-ti—a race of half-human, half-snake creatures—are calculating, suave, and extremely evil. They spend months on battle plans—building elaborate traps, making alliances with other creatures, and using all their considerable intelligence to win a fight before it's even begun.

You may come across many different types of yuan-ti in your travels. A pureblood yuan-ti looks human, but on closer glance, bears a forked tongue, pointed teeth, and patches of scales on its neck and limbs.

*They will build temples in old ruins and occasionally underneath human cities*

## Yuan-ti Facts

| | |
|---|---|
| Maximum Height | 5 to 6 feet |
| Maximum Weight | 200 to 300 pounds |
| Habitat | Warm, forested areas |
| Society | Tribe or nation |
| Diet | Birds |
| Language | Common, Draconic, and Abyssal |
| Attack methods | Poison, spells, acid |
| Best defense | Try blinding them so they can't see you as well |

Yuan-ti disguise themselves as humans and walk among them as spies. A halfblood has more obvious snake features, like a snake's head or tail. A yuan-ti abomination looks like a giant serpent, except for its large muscular arms. Abominations are leaders and extremely gifted spellcasters.

You may have already met a member of this evil race without even knowing it, for all yuan-ti can transform into ordinary snakes. The next time you see a snake, step back. You could be headed for a trap.

# Behir

A behir can slither as smoothly as a viper one moment, then unfold its dozen legs and race ahead with considerable speed. The two large horns on its head and neck appear frightening, but they are actually used for cleaning the creature's hard scales, not for fighting.

A behir doesn't take kindly to human intruders, but its worst enemy is any member of dragonkind. It will stop at nothing to drive a dragon out of its territory.

## Useful Behir Parts

**Horns:** Brew to make ink for lightning bolt scroll

**Talons:** Brew to make ink for neutralize poison scroll

**Heart:** Brew to make ink for energy protection scroll

**Scales:** Extremely hard and beautifully colored; make excellent scale armor

## Behir Facts

| | |
|---|---|
| Maximum Height | 40 feet |
| Maximum Weight | 4,000 pounds |
| Habitat | Cliff faces |
| Society | Solitary |
| Diet | Any living being |
| Language | Common |
| Attack methods | Lightning bolt, swallow whole, constrict |
| Best defense | Stay far away from it and scatter so it has to focus on one of you at a time! |

# Ormyrr

Ormyrrs have enormous grublike bodies that possess powerful arms, a mouthful of extremely sharp teeth, and a surprisingly intelligent brain. They aren't particularly aggressive, tending to keep to themselves.

While (or perhaps because) these creatures have no talent for casting spells, they find magic absolutely irresistible. They will lie, cheat, and steal to obtain a scroll, spellbook, or other magical object, and can be mesmerized by a skillful display of magic powers.

*Block your ears with wax before fighting—its trill can paralyze you!*

## Frost Worm Facts

| | |
|---|---|
| Maximum Height | 40 feet |
| Maximum Weight | 8,000 pounds |
| Habitat | Frozen plains |
| Society | Solitary |
| Diet | Yaks, polar bears, walruses, seals, moose, and mammoths |
| Language | None |
| Attack methods | Trill, cold, breath weapon |
| Best defense | Fire spells work best |

## Ormyrr Facts

| | |
|---|---|
| Maximum Height | 25 feet |
| Maximum Weight | 16 tons |
| Habitat | Muddy riverbanks |
| Society | Solitary or tribes of 6 to 12 |
| Diet | Large fish, crocodiles, hippos and other river dwellers, and raccoons |
| Language | Common |
| Attack methods | Constrict |
| Best defense | Use your best spells to distract it |

*Only occasionally an unlucky human*

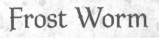

# Frost Worm

A frost worm spends most of its life burrowing through the ice and snow. When it surfaces, it will release a mind-numbing trilling noise from atop its head that will freeze a creature in its tracks. Despite the frost worm's terrifying appearance, people of the frozen wastes have succeeded in training these beasts to protect their tribes, and once trained, the beasts can be ridden using magical, cold-resistant saddles.

# Purple Worm

Distant relatives of frost worms, purple worms inhabit warmer climates. Although I have never come across this creature, I'm told their giant mouth are as big as a human is tall.

## Purple Worm Facts

| | |
|---|---|
| Maximum Height | 80 feet |
| Maximum Weight | 40,000 pounds |
| Habitat | Underground |
| Society | Solitary |
| Diet | Any organic material |
| Language | None |
| Attack methods | Swallow whole, poison |
| Best defense | Cover yourself in grease to make it harder for it to grab you |

# ADDITIONAL DEFENSES

**M**any monsters may seem unbeatable in a head-to-head battle, thanks to their strength, magical prowess, or number of friends. But do not lose heart. Your wit, along with the items on this page, can prove more useful than the traditional blade and bow.

**Steel Mirror**
Helps spot a monster around the corner. Also useful when fighting medusas.

**Hooded Lantern**

**Bullseye Lantern**
Handy when exploring dark dungeons

**Beltpouch**

**Grappling Hook and Rope**

**Torch**

**Smokestick**
Instantly creates a thick, concealing smoke

**Thunderstone**
When thrown, makes a tremendous crashing noise. Will deafen all nearby creatures.

Case for Maps or Scrolls

Tanglefoot Bag
When thrown, the bag will burst open.
The goo inside entangles the beast
and fixes it to the closest surface.

Holy Water
Best used on undead
monsters such as vampires

Sunrod
Creates light for up to six hours

Alchemist's Fire
Instantly catches
fire when thrown

Spellbook

Tools

Acid
Aim for the most vulnerable
part of the monster's body—
typically the eyes

Caltrops
Scatter these in the path of a
pursuing monster—the painful
spikes will slow it down

Spyglass

# SNEAKY SHAPESHIFTERS

These masters of illusion can change form at will—from snarling wolf, to squealing boar or squeaking rat—or in the case of a doppelganger, to the form of your very best friend.

## Werewolf transformation

Eyes glow red in the dark

Thick, shaggy hair

Pointed teeth

Attacks with teeth and claws, and sometimes weapons

Long, strong fingers

Short tail

Wolflike legs

Human

Hybrid

## Werewolf Facts

| | |
|---|---|
| Maximum Height | 6 to 7 feet |
| Maximum Weight | 150 to 200 pounds |
| Habitat | Anywhere |
| Society | Solitary or packs |
| Diet | Meat |
| Language | Common |
| Attack methods | Surprise |
| Best defense | Silver weapons are highly deadly to any werebeast, especially the werewolf |

# Werewolf

The most notorious and lethal of shapeshifters are, of course, werewolves. Werewolves belong to a group of monsters known as lycanthropes. In most cases, lycanthropes are born from the bite of a werewolf. Victims may not realize their unlucky fates until the sight of the full moon transforms them into fearful beasts. Once the transformation is complete, the ability to think as a human disappears, leaving only an animal's thirst for blood. By dawn, the victims return to human form, often with no memory of the incident.

The term "lycanthrope" comes from the root words lycos meaning wolf and anthropos meaning man. However there are many more types of lycanthropes beyond the werewolf. A better term for this group would be "therianthrope," from the root therios (animal).

Natural werewolves do not need a full moon to transform into their monstrous form.

Superior speed

All human traits disappear

Natural werewolves are born from two werewolf parents, while true werewolves are transformed by the bite of another werewolf.

Wolf

Hammocks for cubs

Cooking hearth

Sleeping alcove

Dresser stores human clothes

Seat for "guests"

# TYPICAL WEREWOLF CARAVAN
## Cutaway View

Werewolves can and do have families. The children of werewolf parents are known as natural werewolves. Born in litters, they look like human babies covered in fuzz. They have some wolflike features, such as a snout and sharp teeth, yet have human arms and legs. Cubs remain in the den until they are able to fend for themselves, usually by the age of ten.

True werewolves live in packs of related family members and tend to frequently move from place to place in search of prey. Some make their homes in the wilderness in cavelike dens. Others take over abandoned houses or live in caravans that they drive around the countryside.

Not all werewolves are completely evil. Over time, some control their animal tendencies and live peacefully among other humans. Yet they must always hide their true natures, for if anyone discovered their curse of lycanthropy, they would certainly be driven away.

*This has led to the rumors that many gypsies are in fact werewolves.*

# Werebear

Werewolves only have one natural enemy: werebears. Werebears tend to be good-natured and protective of humans. They tend toward solitary lives, building cabins in the deep woods, where they guard the animals of the region from unwelcome intruders. Werebears will never enter human settlements, except in rare cases to protect the residents from a pack of werewolves.

Werebears seldom have families, but when they do, the male and female remain together only until the children reach maturity. The cubs look identical to human children until the age of eight. At this point, they take on the ability to transform into a big, hairy werebear.

Wearbears tend to be shaggy, stout, and muscular, and the men wear beards. All werebears are grumpy, and their only joy is hunting down evil.

## WEREBEAR FACTS

| | |
|---|---|
| Maximum Height | 8 feet |
| Maximum Weight | 500 pounds |
| Habitat | Cold regions |
| Society | Solitary |
| Diet | Prefer fish, small mammals, and honey-rich mead |
| Language | Common |
| Attack methods | Claws, bite |
| Best defense | Silver weapons |

# Wererat

Known as ratmen, these sleazy beasts are driven by greed. They collect anything they think has any value and ambush humans to steal their gold. Wererats prefer city life, inhabiting the sewers and tunnels beneath the streets. It's easy to spot a wererat in human form for the sewer stench lingers on their clothes.

*Wererats are terrible judges of value. Their hoards are full of more junk than treasure.*

# Wereboar

*Often inhabit sewers beneath cities*

Wereboars are easily angered and just as likely to attack a group of friends as an intruder. In human form, these beasts tend to be stocky, muscular people with short, stiff hair. Wereboars also tend to be rude, and their homes are full of dust and garbage. In spite of their surly personalities, you may find it useful to seek out a wereboar and attempt to forge a friendship. If you succeed, you'll have an invaluable ally and a friend for life.

## Wererat Facts

| | |
|---|---|
| Maximum Height | 2 feet |
| Maximum Weight | 8 pounds |
| Habitat | Any |
| Society | Pack |
| Diet | Will eat anything it can scavenge |
| Language | Common |
| Attack methods | Bite |
| Best defense | Silver weapons |

# Doppelganger

In natural form, doppelgangers appear almost otherworldly. Do not be fooled by their frail appearance: these monsters are hardy, cunning, and determined.

True shapeshifters, these sly beasts can take on the appearance of any human or humanlike creature. By psychically reading minds, they can emulate the exact speech and personality of their victims, fooling even friends and family. Naturally lazy, doppelgangers often select wealthy victims. In other cases the impersonation is part of some larger evil plan. If doppelgangers succeed in killing their victims, they can—and often will—remain in their victims' forms forever.

## Doppelganger Facts

| | |
|---|---|
| Maximum Height | 5½ feet tall |
| Maximum Weight | 150 pounds |
| Habitat | Any |
| Society | Solitary or gang |
| Diet | Anything |
| Language | Common |
| Attack methods | Detect thoughts |
| Best defense | Use true seeing ointment so you don't lose track of it |

## Wereboar Facts

| | |
|---|---|
| Maximum Height | 4 feet |
| Maximum Weight | 500 pounds |
| Habitat | Any dry land |
| Society | Tribes |
| Diet | Small game, vegetables, and fungi |
| Language | Common |
| Attack methods | Bludgeon with tusks |
| Best defense | Silver weapons |

*Especially truffles*

*I've recently learned that the eye of an attavus can substitute for this ointment. Locating and securing such an eye, however, is nearly impossible.*

## True Seeing Ointment

This ointment, when applied to your eyelids, allows you to see the true form of shapeshifters, including doppelgangers.

3 baskets bucolio mushrooms—ground to a fine powder

bushel saffron

1 flask oil of noix

*Only use bucolio mushrooms! Absolutely no substitutions!*

Combine th...

# Gruesome Goblinoids

All goblinoids are related in one way or another to the pesky goblin. Although dim-witted and irritating, these monsters have strength of numbers and a knack for strategy. Underestimate them at your own risk.

Eyes dull and glazed. Become blinded in bright light. Irises vary in color from red to yellow.

Flat face

Broad nose

Small, sharp fangs
Wide mouth

Pointed ears

Arms hang down almost to knees

Often carry short swords, spears, or maces

Some particularly dangerous bands of goblins ride giant wolves into battle.

Skin color depends on tribe: various shades of yellow, orange, deep red

## Goblin Facts

| | |
|---|---|
| Maximum Height | 3 to 3 ½ feet tall |
| Maximum Weight | 40 to 45 pounds |
| Habitat | Typically underground or in ruined cities |
| Society | Tribe |
| Diet | Any creature from rats to humans |
| Language | Goblin |
| Attack methods | Ambush |
| Best defense | Find a narrow bottleneck, so they have to come at you one at a time! |

*However, they eat very little and infrequently.*

*Goblins of above-average intelligence (rare) can speak Common.*

*Use tanglefoot bags to slow them down.*

# Goblin

Stupid and cowardly by nature, goblins thrive only in large numbers. They live, fight, and hunt in big, organized groups. If you encounter a goblin on its own, it's more than likely the dim creature has wandered from its squadron and became lost. Though their sense of strategy is nonexistent, beware any battle with these nasty beasts. Goblins do not fight fairly and will resort to dirty tricks and ambushes—anything that will bring an end to their enemy. You can easily outsmart smaller squadrons of goblins with a simple spell. A larger group is more difficult. But if you do manage to turn the battle against them, they will not hesitate to run.

Because their eyes cannot process bright light, goblins make their homes in underground caverns or the dungeons of ruined towns. They rarely go out in the daytime, except on dark, overcast days.

If you ever find yourself in the realm of a goblin lair, you'll know it by the awful stench. These creatures live in absolute filth and have no need for privacy. They eat and sleep in one large communal space, among the scattered rotting carcasses from previous meals.

In spite of this apparent chaos, goblin society does maintain a strict structure. Goblin warriors fall into bands of about forty, ruled by a single leader. Squadron leaders all report to a chief, who in turn answers to the Goblin King. Kings rise to power based on strength and intelligence, not heredity. In some cases, members of related but more intelligent species—such as hobgoblins or bugbears—will rule a goblin tribe or work closely with a goblin king.

Not all goblins live up to their kind's nasty reputation. I once met a young goblin whose curiosity and intelligence surprised even me. True adventurers never make assumptions about any monster—friend or foe.

Food Store

Slave Pens

Entrance
Passage

Guardroom

Slave
Mine

Junction Cave

Slave
Workshop

Barracks

Goblins'
Communal Area

Chief's
Antechamber

Beetle Farm

Goblin King's
Chamber

Gladiatorial
Pit

Secret
Room

Meeting
Area

Shrine

Hobgoblins'
Quarters

Bugbears'
Quarters

Treasure
Vault

Shaman's
Room

# TYPICAL GOBLIN LAIR
Abandoned Gnome Burrowtown

# Hobgoblin

Hobgoblins hate elves most of all.

Larger, smarter, and more aggressive than their goblin cousins, hobgoblins live for warfare. They spend their lives planning and executing elaborate attacks on elves, humans, and other hobgoblin tribes.

Like goblins, hobgoblins live in communal dwellings underground, sometimes sharing quarters. Hobgoblins, however, consider goblins inferior creatures and often bully them into handing over leadership roles in goblin society.

Hobgoblins sometimes form mercenary bands to fight for evil humanoids.

## Hobgoblin Facts

| | |
|---|---|
| Maximum Height | 6 ½ feet tall |
| Maximum Weight | 400 pounds |
| Habitat | Warm hills. Often in dungeons, caverns, or forests. |
| Society | Tribal |
| Diet | Rotting meat |
| Language | Goblin and Common |
| Attack methods | Ambush |
| Best defense | Find a narrow bottleneck to make them come at you one at a time |

# Bugbear

Although some of my more dim-witted apprentices might claim otherwise, bugbears are not related to bears. The name derives from the appearance of their short snout—capped by a black nose much like a bear's—along with the coarse bearlike fur that covers most of their bodies. These beasts represent the fiercest, largest species of goblinoid known in our world.

Bugbears love mountainous regions. They inhabit networks of caves that extend far underground. They tend to live in smaller groups than their goblin cousins, but still have a rigid social structure in which warriors report to the biggest, most powerful bugbear.

## BUGEAR FACTS

| | |
|---|---|
| Maximum Height | 7 feet |
| Maximum Weight | 500 pounds |
| Habitat | Mountainous regions |
| Society | Tribal |
| Diet | Any creature |
| Language | Goblin and Common |
| Attack methods | Ambush |
| Best defense | Best to gang up on one bugbear at a time |

*including their own kin*

*Known as cubs*

Bugbear young are surprisingly important members of bugbear society. Each tribe has as many young as it has adults, and the cubs learn at a very early age to guard the lair. The young do not join in battles until they are at least thirteen, but they will fight to the death with surprising skill if intruders invade their lair.

Bugbears covet anything shiny and will not pass up an opportunity to increase their hoard of jewels, gold, weapons, and other treasure. If you happen across a bugbear in your journeys, you may avert a conflict simply by tossing a bag of coins into the air.

*Bugbears are crafty and stealthy. Despite their bulk, they are capable of sneaking up on their prey and setting effective ambushes.*

*I've also recently learned that some bugbears have an aversion to large bodies of water, much like cats. I have yet to investigate this for myself.*

# MAMMOTH MONSTERS

Thanks to their incredible size, these mammoth beasts always have the upper hand in a fight. But if you are clever, you can easily win a conflict without ever raising your weapon (or even your wand).

## Troll

Trolls have no fear of death, and with good reason. Not only are they too dim-witted to recognize true threats, but they are able to regrow any body part lost in battle, including their heads. No matter how injured they might be, they will stand up and continue to fight. Trolls are constantly starving and easily distracted. If caught in battle with a troll, tossing a bag of rations in the troll's direction may allow you time to flee the scene.

Trolls cannot regenerate a body part hurt by fire or acid.

| TROLL FACTS | |
|---|---|
| Maximum Height | 9 feet |
| Maximum Weight | 500 pounds |
| Habitat | Prefer cold mountains, but found everywhere |
| Society | Solitary or gang of two to four |
| Diet | Anything from simple grubs to bears and humans |
| Language | Giant |
| Attack methods | Bite, scratch |
| Best defense | Fire and acid; tempt it with a stash of food |

Thick, ropy hair

Walk upright but with
hunched shoulders

Female easily distinguished from
male. She is always larger and
more powerful.

Long powerful hands

Arms dangle free and
drag along the ground

Fingers end in
sharpened claws

Feet have three toes

Well-traveled path

Opening covered with twigs and leaves

Trollholes are always built near trees

Chute to entry

Treasury

Sleeping area

Crude sleeping platforms formed of tree roots

Entry

Bed of soft grass for landing

Communal area

Chieftain's dwelling

## TYPICAL TROLLHOLE
Size of lair varies with size of troll

Trolls live in small gangs of two to four, ruled by a female chieftain. The female acts as the group's spiritual leader and leads their nightly hunts. The group detects prey by using their sharp sense of smell. Once one of the trolls picks up a scent, he or she will howl, and the entire pack will charge in starving frenzy. Any type of meat satiates the group's ravenous appetites, but trolls prefer bears and humans most of all.

Female trolls give birth to a single child every five years or so. Children participate fully in all of the pack's hunts and learn to fight at a very young age. Female children are favored, while males are often treated as servants and made to wait on the chieftain. As young trolls grow older, they may leave the pack to find a lair of their own. Wandering packs are particularly dangerous. They travel at night and sleep by day. All the traveling leaves them ravenous, and they have been known to attack and consume entire villages along the way.

# Ettin

These two-headed giants thrive in filth. They never bathe if they can help it. Their lairs crawl with vermin and stink of rotting food. Ettins generally live alone, but do mate at least once in their lives. The mates remain together only until their child is a few months old. Then the male ettin leaves the female to raise the child by herself. Ettin young grow up remarkably quickly and are ready to leave their mother's side by the age of eight months.

Though stupid and uncivilized, the ettin is a formidable fighter. It always attacks with two clubs, usually covered with spikes. The right head of the ettin serves as the leader of the beast, and its right arm and leg tend to be more muscular and well developed. If you are drawn into conflict with this beast, be sure to attempt to disable the right side first.

*A lone ettin often whiles away the night chatting to itself.*

## Ettin Facts

| | |
|---|---|
| Maximum Height | 13 feet |
| Maximum Weight | 5,200 pounds |
| Habitat | Remote, rocky areas |
| Society | Solitary |
| Diet | Rotting meat |
| Language | A mixture of Orc, Goblin, and Giant |
| Attack methods | Ambush, two-weapon fighting |
| Best defense | Set a trap! An ettin is not very smart |

# Giant

You may believe from legend that these beings are crude and dim-witted, but nothing could be further from the truth. These monsters can be highly intelligent, and rely on brute force to solve problems simply because strength is their greatest weapon. Although considered a single species, giants over the years have evolved into several highly varied races.

*Storm giants build elaborate gardens and prefer to live off the land.*

## Giant Facts

| | |
|---|---|
| Maximum Height | 21 feet tall |
| Maximum Weight | 12,000 pounds |
| Habitat | Various |
| Society | Tribal |
| Diet | Meat and some vegetables |
| Language | Giant and Common |
| Attack methods | Throw rocks |
| Best defense | Their big size makes them slow–try setting a trap or entangling them with a tanglefoot bag and barraging them from afar |

*Or, find a dwarf to fight by your side. Dwarves are expert giant-slayers.*

## Fire Giant

Fire giants resemble large red-haired dwarves. They live in military-like groups ruled by a king or queen, and inhabit volcanic regions or hot springs. These giants adore planning and executing large-scale battles. In combat, they tend to wield flaming swords or throw boulders of smoking, hardened magma at their enemies. At the conclusion of these battles, they often take prisoners, whom they take back to their lair and train as guards.

## Storm Giant

Storm giants resemble gargantuan humans with green skin and flowing green hair. The most intelligent of the giant races, they live in castles built on stormy mountain peaks or underwater. As such, they have evolved the ability to breathe underwater. These gentle beasts shun conflict, preferring to spend their time at home composing or playing music and working in their gardens. However, if sufficiently threatened, they will not hesitate to call upon their powerful spell-casting abilities to defend themselves and their families.

*Very rarely, a storm giant is born with violet skin and deep violet or blue-black hair, and silvery or purple eyes*

## Frost Giant

With light-blue hair and silver skin, frost giants resemble huge, muscular humans. They make their homes in castles or caverns located in regions with significant snowfall. Unlike storm giants, these beasts often have cruel personalities and take pleasure in ambushing passing adventurers by hiding in the snow.

*Tribal leaders call themselves "jarls."*

### A Giant's Bag

Most giants carry a shoulder bag or a belt pouch filled not with gold but with a variety of personal belongings. Inside you might find:

| | | |
|---|---|---|
| Bowl and spoon | Throwing rocks | Dried animal dung |
| Hand-held chopper | Comb | Strong rope |
| Candles | Cooking pot | Shoes |
| Quills and ink | Hairpins | Sewing needle |
| Knife | Chunk of cheese | Beads |
| Wood for whittling | Meat | Cloak |
| Tankard | Musical instrument | Tinderbox |

They have a particular fondness for elf, dwarf, and halfling meat.

## Ogre Facts

| | |
|---|---|
| Maximum Height | 10 feet tall |
| Maximum Weight | 600 to 650 pounds |
| Habitat | Hilly areas |
| Society | Tribe |
| Diet | Anything |
| Language | Giant and Common |
| Attack methods | Smash |
| Best defense | Set a trap or try to lure it to sleep; fight it from a distance! |

# Ogre

Ogres solve problems by smashing them. If they do not succeed in smashing, they will simply run away. Evil-natured and greedy, these beasts often serve as mercenaries to wicked sorcerers in exchange for jewels or gold.

Ogres live in tribes of about eight, loosely ruled by a chieftain, and gather food and treasure by raiding and scavenging neighboring villages. These ugly monsters trust no one—not even members of their own tribe—and frequently erupt into violent arguments over a scrap of rotten meat or a coin found loose in the lair.

They sometimes serve as heavy infantry in orc armies, although they aren't clever tacticians.

# Ogre Mage

Far more intelligent than its cousin the ogre, the ogre mage can easily defeat a foe with a powerful spell. If injured in battle, this beast can rapidly heal itself, including reattaching any lost limbs.

The ogre mage prefers a solitary life, rarely associating with any members of its kind except for members of its own family, known as a clan. The father of a clan wields enormous power over his wife and children, often treating them like slaves. They live together in a fortified structure or an underground lair, and spend their lives trying to amass as much treasure as possible. When a father passes on, the eldest son assumes control of the clan and the treasure.

*If in danger of losing a battle, an ogre mage will turn into a cloud of gas and escape.*

## Ogre Mage Facts

| | |
|---|---|
| Maximum Height | 10 feet |
| Maximum Weight | 700 pounds |
| Habitat | Cold hills |
| Society | Solitary or clans |
| Diet | Fresh meat |
| Language | Giant and Common |
| Attack methods | Spells |
| Best defense | Use acid and fire to stave off its regenerative powers |

*It's resistant to spells.*

Can summon swarms of bats and packs of wolves to do its bidding.

# UNSIGHTLY UNDEAD

The spirits of these monsters have departed the land of the living forever. And yet their bodies, animated by supernatural forces, continue to roam.

## Vampire

Casts no shadow

Of all the undead beasts, vampires are perhaps the most elusive. These creatures walk among us, assuming the form of normal folk. Often their true nature only becomes apparent when they attack.

A vampire lures its victims with false friendship. It might invite you to its home for supper or rescue you from the clutches of another frightful beast. Once alone, the vampire will attempt to gaze into your eyes, as if with deep concern. However, in fact, the vampire's gaze is a type of spell intended to hypnotize you into submission.

Any human, elf, or humanoid beast can be turned into a vampire when cursed with a vampire's bite.

Pale skin

Sharp fangs

Red eyes

Long fingernails

Although technically not considered food, vampires consume blood for the energy life force it delivers.

## VAMPIRE FACTS

| | |
|---|---|
| Maximum Height | 5 to 7 feet |
| Maximum Weight | 200 pounds |
| Habitat | Any |
| Society | Solitary |
| Diet | Blood |
| Language | Any known in life |
| Attack methods | Bite, spells |
| Best defense | Weapons forged of silver are best; wooden stake through the heart to immobilize; prolonged exposure to sunlight kills it |

Vampires will avoid garlic, mirrors, and holy symbols. Poisons and paralysis cannot harm them.

# Typical Vampire Lair

Guest Bedroom

Although their homes often have elaborate master bedroom suites, these rooms are created simply to impress guests. Vampires prefer to do their actual sleeping in dark, out-of-the way areas, such as basements.

Study

Master Bedroom

Second Floor

Living Room

Privy

Kitchen

Library

Stairs to Basement

Dining Room

Coffin

Ground Floor

Vampires live in places that carry a feeling of death and destruction. They make their homes in ruined castles, cemeteries, or abandoned manors. Vampires enjoy a life of finery and often decorate their homes with lavish furniture and expensive artwork gathered from their victims. The lair serves as a safe haven from the rising sun. Vampires die when exposed to sunlight and therefore spend the daylight hours sleeping, usually in a coffin.

Basement

Vampires have the power to transform at will into bats (or wolves) and into a gaseous mist.

Vampires tend to live alone, but will, on occasion, form family groups. These groups usually are made up of a vampire lord and several of his past victims who have become vampires themselves. These newer vampires serve the vampire lord's wishes, gathering food for the family or performing simple tasks in the world of the living. When the vampire lord dies, the other vampires depart from the lair to continue their lives alone.

As powerful as these beings may be, there are many means to avert their attacks. Vampires despise the odor of garlic and will not come near the scent. They are also repelled by holy symbols and mirrors. These monsters cannot cross running water, but they can travel on a ship as long as they are resting. No vampire can enter a private home or building without an invitation from someone living there. The best escape from a vampire, therefore, may be within your own home.

Vampires can pass freely in community buildings and other public places like libraries, as these are open to all.

I received this letter from one of my old adventuring companions, recounting his shocking experience with a vampire in mist-form.

The thick mist appeared without warning, seeming to rise from the ground like a foul exhalation. At first we paid it little mind; at night, ground fogs are fairly common. But then we noticed how the fog was moving, swirling toward us even though there was no wind to drive it. What could we do? How can we fight a fog?

It was then that the leading tendril wrapped itself around Batlas Pre...

## Ghost Facts

| | |
|---|---|
| Maximum Height | Whatever it was in life |
| Maximum Weight | None |
| Habitat | Any |
| Society | Solitary |
| Diet | None |
| Language | Any used in life |
| Attack methods | Supernatural fear, life-draining touch |
| Best defense | Don't look it in the eyes, and plug your ears with wax; its gaze and moan have frightened many adventurers |

*It hates holy water, holy spells, and blessed weapons.*

# Ghost

A ghost haunts the places that it once frequented in life. It is quite rare to come across a ghost. Normally, the ghost returns with a *Most often to seek revenge* purpose and will only appear to the person it plans to haunt. However, if you do come across one, remember your ability to defeat a ghost has little to do with powerful spells or brute force. The best defense is simply to set right whatever situation caused the spirit to become trapped in the mortal world.

# Zombie

A complicated spell performed by an evil wizard brings these putrid monsters to life. The zombies act as slaves, following their master's every command. They move at a slow, jerky pace with their arms outstretched, and they cannot think on their own. The wizard who created the beasts must remain in their presence to command these monsters, and the commands must be no more than a few simple words. *Go there! Kill that monster! And so on.*

# Ghoul

With sharp teeth, sunken eye sockets, and a virtually hairless head, this beast looks like the walking dead. A ghoul is a human transformed into a monster by the bite of another ghoul. Once transformed, a ghoul has recognizable human body parts and features, however its mind has lost all reason.

## Zombie Facts

| | |
|---|---|
| Maximum Height | Whatever it was in life |
| Maximum Weight | None |
| Habitat | Prefers graveyards |
| Society | Solitary or pack |
| Diet | None |
| Language | Cannot talk |
| Attack methods | Whatever they were skilled at in life |
| Best defense | They are very slow— as long as they have to run after you they can never attack you |

*Use slashing weapons like a saber*

## Ghoul Facts

| | |
|---|---|
| Maximum Height | Varies |
| Maximum Weight | None |
| Habitat | Graveyards, battlefields |
| Society | Solitary |
| Diet | Carrion |
| Language | Any used in life |
| Attack methods | Ambush from behind gravestones or burst from shallow graves. |
| Best defense | Make it come to you— always make it move |

*Delivers ghoul fever. The victim of a bite gets a fever, dies, then rises the next day as a ghoul.*

# Nightwalker

Taller than a house and made up of pure darkness, the nightwalker lurks in the shadows of the evening hours. Vaguely humanoid in shape, it wears no clothing and has a smooth hairless body. It can crush a weapon simply by picking it up and frighten a foe to death with one evil look. This strong spellcaster can also call forth an army of other undead to serve its evil plans.

## Nightwalker Facts

| | |
|---|---|
| Maximum Height | 20 feet tall |
| Maximum Weight | None |
| Habitat | Any |
| Society | Solitary |
| Diet | None |
| Language | None |
| Attack methods | Ambush from the darkness |
| Best defense | Use silver weapons and spells of bright light. (It is immune to cold and resistant to other spells) |

*It hates holy magic and blessed weapons.*

## LICH FACTS

| | |
|---|---|
| Maximum Height | Whatever it was in life |
| Maximum Weight | Whatever it was in life |
| Habitat | Strong keep or subterranean crypt |
| Society | Solitary |
| Diet | None |
| Language | Common plus any languages known in life |
| Attack methods | Various spells, paralyzing touch |
| Best defense | Discover the lich's true name; destroy its phylactery |

## Lich

Obsessed with power, this undead spellcaster works relentlessly on schemes that may take years, or even centuries. In life, a lich may have been a well-known wizard, but once transformed, the creature loses all memory of its former identity. Few liches even recall their true names and instead take on honorifics such as "The Black Hand" or "The Forgotten King." Discover the lich's true name, and it will have no choice but to follow your commands.

*Liches live forever, so they can afford to be patient. They have all the time in the world to enact their plans.*

### A Lich's Phylactery

A wizard can only become a lich by choice, following a precise set of steps:

1. Create a phylactery. The phylactery may take the form of a box, an amulet, or a ring, depending on the wizard's style and personality. Most common: a sealed metal box containing magical phrases written on strips of parchment.

2. Craft a life-force potion. The recipe for this potion is kept under lock and key at the Wee Jas Library.

2. At the next full moon, imbibe the potion. The drinker's life-force drains into the enchanted phylactery.

3. The transformation begins.

*Apprentices: Do NOT attempt to retrieve! That means you, Kellach!*

## Mummy Facts

| | |
|---|---|
| Maximum Height | 5 or 6 feet |
| Maximum Weight | 120 pounds |
| Habitat | Dry desert areas, tombs, or temple complexes |
| Society | Solitary or squad |
| Diet | None *But mummies seldom bother to speak.* |
| Language | Common |
| Attack methods | Paralyze victims with fear, infect with mummy rot |
| Best defense | Fire, holy spells, and blessed weapons |

# Mummy

In dry, desert areas, people preserve the dead by a process known as mummification.

After removing the brain, heart, and liver, the body is soaked in a preserving solution and covered with spices and resins, then wrapped in hundreds of yards of cloth.

A mummy shambles out and attacks when a graverobber disturbs its treasure-filled crypt. Supernaturally strong, mummies are difficult to conquer. The mere sight of one causes despair in some adventurers. Others may find themselves infected with mummy rot, a disease that causes a body to instantly rot away. The best recourse is to stay far away from tombs. *Or, perhaps, resist the urge to plunder them*

*Or overly curious apprentice*

## Shadow Facts

| | |
|---|---|
| Maximum Height | 6 feet |
| Maximum Weight | None |
| Habitat | Ancient ruins, graveyards, and dungeons |
| Society | Roving bands |
| Diet | None |
| Language | None |
| Attack methods | Life-draining touch |
| Best defense | Use holy magic and blessed weapons |

## Skeleton Facts

| | |
|---|---|
| Maximum Height | Varies |
| Maximum Weight | Varies |
| Habitat | Any |
| Society | Groups |
| Diet | None |
| Language | None |
| Attack methods | Skeletal claws; rusty weapons |
| Best defense | Use bludgeoning weapons |

# Skeleton

Skeletons serve evil wizards, who create them to act as warriors or guards. They have no muscles or ligaments; their bones move purely through magic. Like zombies, they take action only after receiving simple commands from the wizard who created them. They typically rove an area in large groups. When a skeleton dies, its bones fall apart and scatter on the ground.

But do not assume it is safe to pass.
The wizard can easily recreate his warrior.

# Shadow

Shadows specialize in terrifying their victims. With a chilling touch, they can drain the life-force of passersby and turn them into shadows as well. Shadows lurk in the darkness of graveyards, ruins, and dungeons. They have no leaders or evil schemes, and no one knows why they exist or where they came from.

My research indicates they were magically created before the War, but I cannot confirm.

# Armor

The monsters in the next two chapters are some of the most fearsome you may ever encounter. If you do happen to meet these vile beasts, do not, under any circumstance, attempt to defend yourself unprepared. True adventurers know to select the proper armor before embarking on any quest. The type you choose depends on your strength as well as the kinds of monsters you may face along the way.

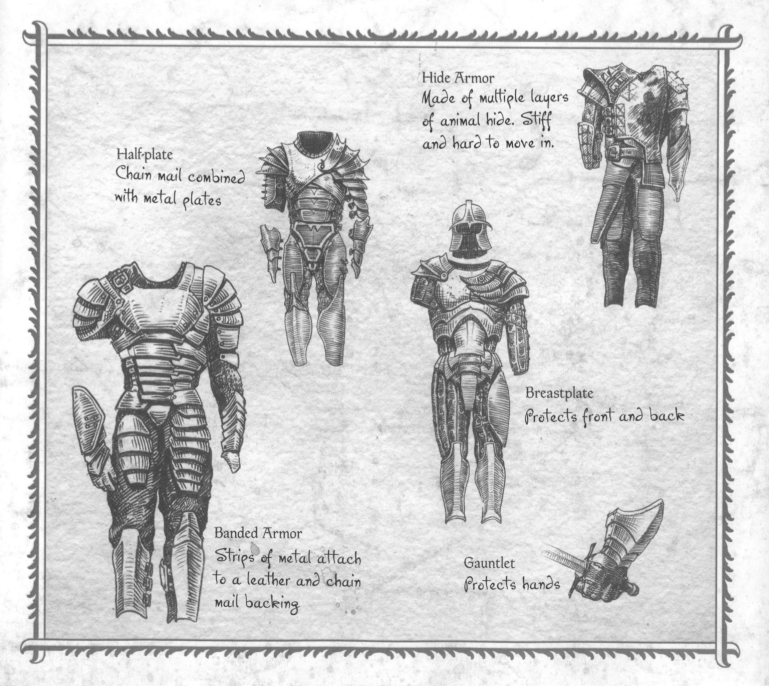

**Hide Armor**
Made of multiple layers of animal hide. Stiff and hard to move in.

**Half-plate**
Chain mail combined with metal plates

**Breastplate**
Protects front and back

**Banded Armor**
Strips of metal attach to a leather and chain mail backing

**Gauntlet**
Protects hands

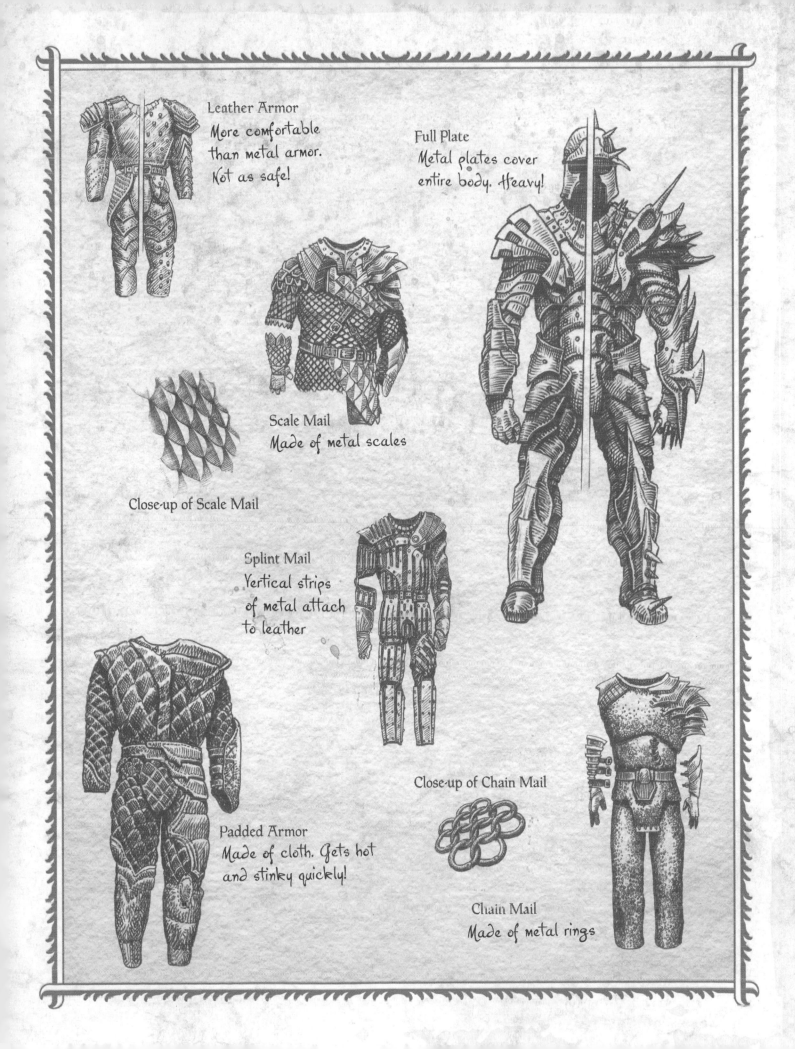

Leather Armor
More comfortable than metal armor. Not as safe!

Full Plate
Metal plates cover entire body. Heavy!

Scale Mail
Made of metal scales

Close-up of Scale Mail

Splint Mail
Vertical strips of metal attach to leather

Close-up of Chain Mail

Padded Armor
Made of cloth. Gets hot and stinky quickly!

Chain Mail
Made of metal rings

A beholder's skin is tough, stony, and about as durable as metal. In death, beholder's skin hardens into a lump of stone.

Each eye has the ability to cast a different kind of spell by shooting a ray of energy at the beholder's victim.

Central eye produces an anti-magic energy cone that will render any spells useless (including its own). The beholder activates the cone by opening its central eye.

Large teeth made for ripping, tearing, and grinding

A beholder's body is naturally buoyant in air. It can float slowly about wherever it wishes. When sleeping, the body floats in place.

A beholder's eyestalks are flexible tentacles about half the body's diameter in length. Beholders can pick up and carry small items—including magic wands—by wrapping their eyestalks around them.

Favorites include small mammals and rodents; mushrooms; roast beef, lamb, or pork; and liver pate. Least favorites: hard-boiled eggs, grapes, or eyes.

## Beholder Facts

| | |
|---|---|
| Maximum Height | 8 feet |
| Maximum Weight | 600 pounds |
| Habitat | Underground caverns |
| Society | Solitary or hives |
| Diet | Anything |
| Language | Beholder and Common |
| Attack methods | Spells, bite |
| Best defense | Disable the eyes |

Once blinded, a beholder can no longer aim its eye rays well enough to properly attack.

# AWFUL ABERRATIONS

Aberrations are quite possibly the strangest monsters in our world. These are the beasts with such bizarre anatomy that they can be classified no other way.

## Beholder

Arrogant and aggressive, beholders hate all creatures that are not exactly like themselves, including other kinds of beholders. They attack without cause. There are many varieties and subspecies of beholders, but each group believes themselves to be the "true" representation of the species.

Beholders are also known as Eye Tyrants.

## TYPICAL BEHOLDER LAIR
Size of lair varies with size of beholder

Typically hobgoblins, goblins, humans, or dwarves

Beholders construct elaborate lairs using their disintegrate rays to forge tunnels through rock. They design their lairs to be particularly difficult to locate. There is only a single entrance, left raw and unsculpted so that it looks like a natural crevice.

Beholders live alone or in hives of five to ten. The monsters typically share their lairs with several minions whom they have enslaved to gather food and guard the dwelling. A hive mother rules over the minions and the hive's younger beholders, who are usually her own children or distant relatives. Called the "Ultimate Tyrant," a hive mother is about twice the size of a normal beholder and has a full set of eyes, but no eyestalks.

Beholder lairs often have vertical passages as well as horizontal ones. Since beholders float, they have no trouble navigating vertical tunnels.

## Typical Beholder Lair Key

1. **Vestibule**
   Barely sculpted by beholder to keep entry as secret as possible

2. **Slither Tunnel**
   Allows beholder minion to monitor the entry

3. **Gauntlet**
   Uneven flooring–often contains a dangerous pit trap

4. **False Central Gallery**
   Typically contains once-human statues, victims turned to stone by the beholder's eye ray. Trap doors allow minions to surprise attacking intruders

5. **Second Gauntlet**
   Usually contains a secret door built into the rock

6. **Central Gallery**
   The "living room" of the beholder's lair

7. **Midden**
   Used by beholder to dump its trash

8. **Minion Chambers**
   Slaves sleep here

9. **The Secret Heart**
   The beholder's private chambers

10. **Escape Chute**
    Usually capped by a boulder to protect privacy

These notes are taken from Ronassic of Sigil's journal. The great scholar once lived in disguise in a beholder hive until he was caught and barely escaped with his life.

Kakwatt translates roughly to the word "punk" in Common.

A beholder gives birth to live young, known as kakwatt in the Beholder language. On the morning of a birth, the community lines up and waits for the mother and newborn to float past. The bystanders inspect the child for any defects. If it does not pass the test, it is destroyed immediately.

Despite their barbaric personalities, beholders have developed an artistic culture. They take great pride in the architecture of their lairs— master builders hold a place of honor in their society. They enjoy sculpting using their telekinesis powers and their eyes' disintegrate rays. They gather together on a regular basis to tell elaborate stories of their victories over other species.

## Typical Beholder Day

**5:30 AM** Awaken and inspect lair for signs of intruders.

**6:30 AM** Float through sleep caves of minions; loudly promise death to all who do not awaken.

**7:00 AM** Go to library or laboratory and continue current research.

**12:00 PM** Sneak up on minions and make sure they are performing their duties. Frighten slackers.

**12:30 PM** Enjoy the daily meal prepared by a minion.

**1:00 PM** Work on master plan. Float throughout lair for hours and mumble while finalizing details and speculating on enemy responses.

**6:00 PM** Prepare for exit. Endlessly grill the scouts and other minions on their mission. Make sure their puny minds have retained some portion of their orders.

**7:00 PM** Exit the lair. Scout the local region and observe humans in their activities. Note details of specific areas of interest.

**12:00 AM** Lead a raid on a home, bookshop, temple, or ruin. Collect needed information for research.

**1:00 AM** Return to lair. Catalog findings, add to the map, and dictate communications to

# Ettercap

At first glance, an ettercap appears to be a human cursed with a spider's features. But upon closer inspection, it is clear that the ettercap is more monster than man. Its humanlike mouth houses venomous fangs and a hollow tongue for sipping the blood of its prey. Its clawed hands have no thumbs and only two fingers, but still the beast manages quite well, using its fangs to assist in picking up small objects.

A gland in an ettercap's abdomen secretes a silky substance that can be woven into webs, much like a spider's. The ettercap spins an elaborate network of traps near well-traveled forest paths to trap passersby.

## CHUUL FACTS

| | |
|---|---|
| Maximum Height | 8 feet |
| Maximum Weight | 650 pounds |
| Habitat | Swamps and jungles |
| Society | Solitary |
| Diet | Intelligent prey |
| Language | Common |
| Attack methods | Constricts, paralytic tentacles |
| Best defense | Don't get too close–fire arrows and spells at it from afar |

## ETTERCAP FACTS

| | |
|---|---|
| Maximum Height | 6 feet |
| Maximum Weight | 200 pounds |
| Habitat | Forests |
| Society | Solitary |
| Diet | Prefer still-living flesh |
| Language | Common |
| Attack methods | Paralyzing poison, web |
| Best defense | Use fire on the webs |

Ettercaps love spiders and keep smaller species as pets.

## Chuul

Chuuls are lobsterlike beasts that rise from the shallows of the waters to attack. They will grasp their prey with strong claws, squeezing it tight, then poison it with their tentacles. Although amphibious, chuuls are actually poor swimmers and prefer life on land.

## Otyugh

The otyugh lives in piles of garbage. Covering itself with rotting meat and other trash, it leaves only its sensory stalk exposed. It will remain hidden for days, relentlessly shoveling garbage into its mouth. A shy monster by nature, it will not attack unless starving or directly threatened.

*Beware an otyugh's bite. Those bitten by an otyugh often contract filth fever.*

### OTYUGH FACTS

| | |
|---|---|
| Maximum Height | 8 feet |
| Maximum Weight | 500 pounds |
| Habitat | Under garbage heaps |
| Society | Solitary |
| Diet | Rotting meat and all manner of trash |
| Language | Common |
| Attack methods | Constrict |
| Best defense | Toss it food and run past! |

# Rust Monster

Although this beast does not directly threaten passersby, most adventurers avoid it at all costs, for it can destroy weapons and armor with a single strike. About the size of a pony, the rust monster has four segmented legs and a compact body protected by a thick hide. Two antennae, one extending from beneath each eye, serve as the monster's prime defense.

A rust monster can pick up the scent of metal from nearly one hundred feet away and will charge until it reaches the source (usually a shield, piece of armor, or sword). Do not bother to run. If you do, the creature will make chase and will not give up until it has its prize. Instead, try tossing a few unnecessary metal objects in the monster's path to distract it long enough to make your escape.

## Rust Monster Facts

| | |
|---|---|
| Maximum Height | 3 feet |
| Maximum Weight | 200 pounds |
| Habitat | Underground |
| Society | Solitary |
| Diet | Metal |
| Language | None |
| Attack methods | Rust |
| Best defense | Throw it some metal to keep it happy |

Use nonmetal weapons and armor, or keep your distance and fight it from afar.

## Grick Facts

| | |
|---|---|
| Maximum Height | 8 feet |
| Maximum Weight | 200 pounds |
| Habitat | Dungeons and caves |
| Society | Solitary or cluster |
| Diet | Anything that moves |
| Language | None |
| Attack methods | Tentacles |
| Best defense | Use a net or a tanglefoot bag to stick it in place |

## ATHACH FACTS

| | |
|---|---|
| Maximum Height | 18 feet |
| Maximum Weight | 4,500 pounds |
| Habitat | Hills |
| Society | Solitary, gang, or tribe |
| Diet | Mountain goats and other fresh meat |
| Language | Giant |
| Attack methods | Pound, poisonous bite |
| Best defense | Use archery and spells to shoot it from afar; spread out in a circle so it can only hit one of you at a time |

# Athach

You can always smell an athach coming, for the beast rarely—if ever—bathes. Extremely strong and extremely stupid, this monster relies on its might to win a battle. Although at first glance it may appear to be a giant, the third arm extending from its chest quickly distinguishes it from its giant cousins.

Athachs actually hate and fear other giants and most things bigger than them.

# Grick

With four tentacles a little longer than a human's forearms, a grick will lash out at anything that moves. These monsters live underground, in spaces that can house their wormlike bodies: burrows, holes, ledges, and crevices. But when hungry, they will venture above ground to find food.

# Otherworldly Outsiders

Rakshasas have the ability to read the thoughts of their victims and gain their trust. They often disguise themselves to make that trust more secure.

Outsiders originate in worlds and planes of existence outside our own. How they flit between their worlds and ours is a mystery I have yet to understand.

## Rakshasa

Although this race of monsters comes from a realm other than our own, rakshasas are commonly found in our world, launching schemes to destroy humanoid settlements. Masters of sorcery and illusion, these beasts use their psychic abilities to shape-change into more innocent-looking beings in order to set their plans in motion. They often take on the appearance of nobles, for rakshasas adore living life in luxury.

Rakshasas always wear expensive clothing. They prefer clothes made of rich fabrics like silk, satin, and cashmere, and often complement their clothing with elaborate jewelry.

## Rakshasa Facts

| | |
|---|---|
| Maximum Height | 6 to 7 feet |
| Maximum Weight | 250 to 300 pounds |
| Habitat | Human settlements, Rakshasa realms |
| Society | Solitary |
| Diet | Fresh human meat |
| Language | Common, Infernal, and Undercommon |
| Attack methods | Spells |
| Best defense | Use blessed crossbow bolts; use true seeing ointment or glitterdust to see him if he turns invisible |

A rakshasa bears the striped fur of a tiger and a tigerlike head. Its body is otherwise vaguely humanoid.

Sharp fangs make for a powerful bite

Sharp claws lash out at foes

A rakshasa has thumbs on the outside of its hands, rather than the interior like humans. Very disturbing!

# TYPICAL RAKSHASA PALACE
Ground floor

## Typical Rakshasa Palace Key

1. Banquet Hall
2. Kitchen and Pantries
3. Smoking Room
4. Dining Room
5. State Drawing Room
6. Major Council Chamber
7. Butler's Library
8. Conservatory
9. Visiting Servants' Quarters
10. Closet
11. Butler's Room
12. Guest Sitting Room
13. East Court
14. Entertainers' Quarters
15. General Sitting Room
16. Trophy Room
17. Stage
18. Bath
19. Ballroom
20. Vestibule
21. Entryway
22. Servants' Quarters
23. West Court
24. State Guest Chamber
25. Gallery
26. Courtyard
27. Tanadar's Room
28. Patio
29. Garden Loggia

## Rakshasa Castes

Rakshasas tend to live a solitary life in our world. However, in their own realms, rakshasas live together in communities divided into strict social classes, known as castes. A rakshasa is born into a caste, and that caste will never change.

Brahmin: The top tier—usually priests and families of great heroes

Kshatriya: Nobles

Vaishya: Common folk, merchants, craftspeople

Shudra: Poor folk, farmers—the absolute bottom of the ladder; considered by other castes to be easily replaceable

Rakshasa love luxury and construct elaborate palaces as their homes. Rakshasa young—known as cubs—grow at the same pace as humans. A single cub is born to a rakshasa mother, and raised until approximately the age of twenty, when it strikes out on its own. Rakshasa culture favors males, therefore male births prompt elaborate celebrations, while female births are merely accepted grudgingly. Unlike humans, however, rakshasas are virtually immortal and only need to create a new generation about once a century.

## Nightmare Facts

| | |
|---|---|
| Maximum Height | 6 feet  *at shoulder* |
| Maximum Weight | 1000 pounds |
| Habitat | Anywhere |
| Society | Solitary |
| Diet | None |
| Language | None |
| Attack methods | Flaming hooves, poison smoke |
| Best defense | Attack it on a windy day so its poisonous smoke disperses |

# Nightmare

If a black horse crosses your path, proceed with caution. At first glance, it appears to be nothing more than a handsome black steed, but upon closer look you observe the burning hooves, glowing black eyes, flaming nostrils, and fiery mane of a true monster: the nightmare.

Nightmares serve the bidding of deeply evil masters—from dark wizards to dangerous demons. Although they have no wings, nightmares can fly at lightning speeds. They roam the world enacting their masters' evil schemes and haunting the dreams of any who try to stand in their way.

## Xorn Facts

| | |
|---|---|
| Maximum Height | 8 feet |
| Maximum Weight | 9,000 pounds |
| Habitat | Underground |
| Society | Solitary or cluster |
| Diet | Precious metals and minerals |
| Language | Common and Terran |
| Attack methods | Ambush from below ground |
| Best defense | Use acid, sonic, and bludgeoning weapons |

## Azer Facts

| | |
|---|---|
| Maximum Height | 4½ feet |
| Maximum Weight | 170 pounds |
| Habitat | Elemental plane of fire |
| Society | Clan |
| Diet | Charred meat |
| Language | Ignan and Common |
| Attack methods | Spear or hammer |
| Best defense | Don't touch it or use metal weapons—it'll superheat any metal you touch it with. Use cold spells; it's vulnerable to cold. |

# Azer

Rare but fascinating beasts, azers occupy the plane of fire, only entering our world on obsessive quests for gems. Similar to dwarves, but with flaming hair and burning hot skin, these creatures can sear a foe with a touch. You will very rarely encounter an azer alone. If you do find one, take heed: the beast will most likely be lost and desperate, and therefore incredibly fierce.

# Xorn

For an adventurer, this monster may be nothing more than a curiosity. Possibly one of the most bizarre-looking creatures you may encounter, its entire head is made up of a fang-filled mouth, surrounded by three arms and several eyes that can see in any direction. Xorns rarely attack living beings. The exception is the adventurer with treasure. You see, xorns crave precious metals. With their incredibly sharp sense of smell, these beasts can sense the presence of metal from as far as twenty feet away and will chase down any creature in order to steal the hoard away.

## Couatl Facts

| | |
|---|---|
| Maximum Height | 12 feet |
| Maximum Weight | 1,800 pounds |
| Habitat | Warm, junglelike areas |
| Society | Solitary |
| Diet | Sloths, possums, and other medium-sized rodents |
| Language | Common, Celestial, and Draconic |
| Attack methods | Poison, spells |
| Best defense | Use glitterdust or trueseeing ointment to make it visible, and a net to hold it still |

*Couatls can shift planes, shift forms, and turn invisible at will, making them very hard to hold on to if they don't want to be caught.*

# Couatl

According to some sources, this flying serpentine beast shares a common ancestor with dragons. After my years of research into the matter, I was unable to find any definitive proof to confirm this conjecture. However it's not difficult to see where this rumor may have begun.

Highly intelligent—like dragons—the couatl rarely attacks without some provocation. But when angered it will not hesitate to unleash a maelstrom of spells from the air. Couatls mate for life, but only have a child once per century. The young reach maturity after thirty years, though some will choose to remain with their parents for up to a hundred years.

Couatls can be persuaded to help adventurers in need, but if you do seek this creature's advice, be certain your needs are truly pressing. If sought for frivolous reasons, the couatl will at best fly away. At worst—I'll leave that to your imagination.

Complete this examination as the final test of your wizarding education. Record your answers on a separate parchment scroll and deliver the results to the Tower of Sorcery. If you have selected the correct answers, you will be rewarded with your wizard's robes. Good luck.

1. Which creepy crawler eats its prey whole?
   Bulette      Phase Spider

2. Which outsider doesn't eat meat?
   Xorn         Rakshasa

3. A chimera never eats plants.
   True         False

4. Crimini mushrooms may be used in a spell of true seeing.
   True         False

5. All mammoth monsters are stupid.
   True         False

6. When you come across a rust monster, the best defense is to run.
   True         False

7. How many monsters in this volume would you consider a potential friend or ally?

   0     5     10     15     All

Text by
Nina Hess

Edited by
Stacy Whitman

Cover art by
Emily Fiegenschuh

Interior art by
Emily Fiegenschuh, Beth Trott, Eva Widermann, and Sam Wood

Cartography by
Lee Moyer, Shane Nitzsche, and Emily Fiegenschuh

Art Direction by
Kate Irwin

Graphic Design by
Lisa Hanson

Special thanks to Ken Cooke, Susan Morris, Chris Perkins,
Ben Schuh, Carter Wyatt, and James Wyatt.

To read more adventures featuring these and other monsters, ask for the Knights of the Silver Dragon series at your local bookstore, starting with *Secret of the Spiritkeeper* by Matt Forbeck. And don't miss *A Practical Guide to Dragons*.

Visit our web site at **www.mirrorstonebooks.com**

A Practical Guide to Monsters
©2007 Wizards.

All characters in this book are fictitious. Any resemblance to actual persons, living or dead, is purely coincidental.
This book is protected under the copyright laws of the United States of America. Any reproduction or unauthorized use of the material or artwork contained herein is prohibited without the express written permission of Wizards of the Coast, Inc.

Published by Wizards of the Coast, Inc. MIRRORSTONE, and its logo is a trademark of Wizards of the Coast, Inc., in the U.S.A. and other countries.

Ronassic of Sigil's notes originally published in Aaron Allston's definitive text on beholder behavior: *I, Tyrant* © TSR 1996.
Batlas's demise originally published in *Van Richten's Guide to Vampires* © TSR 1991.

Printed in the U.S.A.
First Printing: August 2007
Library of Congress Cataloging-
in-Publication Data is available
9 8 7 6 5 4 3 2
US ISBN:978-0-7869-4809-3
620-95989720-001-EN

U.S., CANADA, ASIA, PACIFIC,
& LATIN AMERICA
Wizards of the Coast, Inc.
P.O. Box 707
Renton, WA 98057-0707
+1-800-324-6496

EUROPEAN HEADQUARTERS
Hasbro UK Ltd
Caswell Way
Newport, Gwent NP9 0YH
GREAT BRITIAN
Please keep this address for your records.